CATS
AND KITTENS

ROSE HILL

Watch the cat run

Hold the book like this.

Watch the top right hand corner and flick the pages over fast.

watch here

Being a cat owner

Before you get a cat, there are some important things to think about. First, make sure that everyone at home agrees to have a pet.

A cat can live for 15 years. You will have to look after it every day. Never abandon a cat – in some countries it's against the law.

If you go away for more than a day, you will have to make sure someone else can feed and look after the cat.

Your cat will need your company. It will enjoy being stroked by you. Cats purr when they are happy. They are friendly if they are looked after properly.

Keeping a cat can be expensive. Food, vet's bills, and stays in a cattery all cost money.

(But sometimes your cat will want to be alone.)

Cats are exciting to watch. They move beautifully. They don't need to be taken for a walk, but they do like to go out by themselves. It's unfair to get a cat if you live on a busy road or by a railway. Why do you think this is?

Cats are related to wild cats like lions and tigers. They like to hunt outside.

If you have another pet

You should always keep any fishes or small pet animals away from your cat's reach. Small animals may die of fright.

Don't leave a cat and dog together until they have got used to each other. Then they may become friends.

3

Getting a cat

It's best to choose your kitten when it is still with its mother. You can find your kitten through advertisements, friends, the vet or a local animal welfare society. Never take a cat from the street. It may have a good home somewhere.

Long-haired cats need a lot of grooming.

Pedigree cats are bred for their looks. They are expensive to buy and may need a lot of care and attention.

You can take a kitten home when it is 8 weeks old. Kittens grow quickly. When they are very young, you can tell their age by what they do:

1. When kittens are only a few hours old they can't see or walk.

2. After 8-10 days, their eyes are open and they can walk.

3. At 4 weeks they can climb out of the "nest".

4. By the time they are 5-6 weeks old, they become daring and play with anything.

5. After 8 weeks, they no longer need their mother's milk. They eat solid food.

How to choose a kitten

When you choose from a family of kittens, watch them all for as long as possible. Try to pick the kitten with the brightest eyes that is also clean, curious and playful. It must be able to run properly. Check that the mother is healthy as well.

All kittens are different. Some are strong and active.

Some are timid and take longer to learn.

Others are curious and may get into trouble.

Your kitten's new home

Before you bring your kitten home, there are seven things you should have ready. They are shown on these two pages.

1. You will need a basket or box to carry your kitten home in. A strong cardboard box will do but it must be tightly shut.

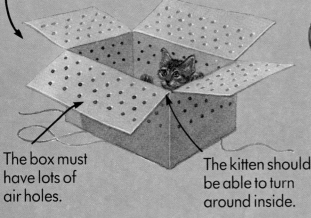

The box must have lots of air holes.

The kitten should be able to turn around inside.

2. You will need three bowls for food, water and milk.

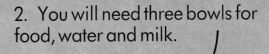

4. You could buy or make a few toys for your kitten to play with.

cooking foil

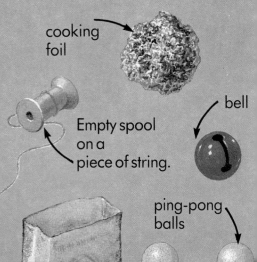

bell

Empty spool on a piece of string.

3. Your kitten will need a litter tray indoors because it will not be able to go outside at first. Don't put the tray next to its bed or its food.

newspaper

Fill the tray with sand, earth or a cat litter bought from a supermarket or a pet store.

ping-pong balls

paper bags

blanket

Low entrance for kitten.

old magazines

5. You will need a brush and a metal comb. If you groom your kitten when it is young, it will soon get used to being brushed.

Wooden post covered in sacking.

Raise the bed a little way off the ground to keep the kitten warm and out of draughts.

6. Give your kitten a bed in a warm, quiet place. You could use a basket or a cardboard box with a blanket inside.

The post is nailed to a wooden base.

You will have to train a young kitten to use a scratching post. Hold its paw and scratch the post gently.

7. Cats need to sharpen their claws. If there is nothing else, your kitten may scratch the furniture. Give it a piece of soft wood instead, or get someone to help you make a scratching post like this one. You can also buy special boards to hang on the wall.

Your kitten may be timid at first. But after a few days, it will become bolder and more curious. When it has settled down, take it to the vet for a check up. Ask about injections against diseases and about neutering (see page 22).

7

Feeding cats and kittens

Cats and kittens are fussy eaters. You can feed them on fresh foods, or on good quality tinned cat and kitten foods, or on a mixture of both.

When your kitten begins to eat solid food, give it 4 small meals a day. When it is 4 months old, start cutting down the number of meals to 3 larger ones a day. When it is about 8 months old, it should need only 2 larger meals a day.

Kittens need good food to grow strong and healthy. The easiest way to feed a kitten is to give it good quality tinned kitten food. You can also feed it on fresh foods (meat, fish, breakfast cereal, brown bread and milk). Ask your vet about vitamins and minerals and for advice about a balanced diet for your kitten. Never give a cat tinned dog food.

Give your kitten **milk** every mealtime until it is 4 months old. Older kittens should have milk only once or twice a day. Fully grown cats don't really need milk but they may like a little sometimes. Some cats don't like milk. **All cats and kittens need water.** Always leave fresh water out for your pet so that it can drink whenever it wants to.

8

Cats and kittens like to be fed at the same time every day, in the same quiet corner. A short while after the cat has finished eating, take the bowl away and wash it.

Chicken bones

Even well-fed cats will steal food.

Don't let your cat have any small, sharp bones like chicken bones. They might make the cat choke. Wrap the bones up and put them in a bin with a tight-fitting lid.

Teeth

Cats are mainly meat-eaters. They have long, sharp canine teeth for tearing meat. Their cheek teeth are used to cut the meat up into small pieces. A kitten can't cut up its own food.

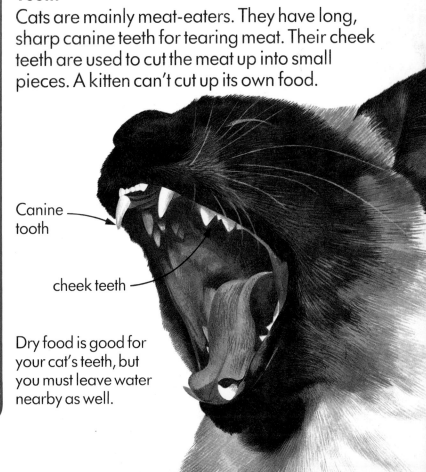

Canine tooth

cheek teeth

Dry food is good for your cat's teeth, but you must leave water nearby as well.

Sleeping

Cats sleep about 15 hours a day. You can give your cat its own bed, but it will sleep wherever it wants to.

They like to sleep in warm places.

They like tight places to squeeze themselves into.

Sometimes they pick odd places.

They like to sleep in hidden places. Before you close a door, make sure the cat isn't inside.

Cats often sleep lightly. Their ears can pick up sounds and they can wake up quickly.

Sometimes cats sleep soundly. They will sleep like this only when they feel safe. They often curl right round in a ball. If the cat dreams, it may twitch and make little noises.

When cats wake up, they stretch their bodies.

They may yawn first.

They stretch their front legs.

They stretch their back legs.

Then they arch their back right up like this.

Don't put your cat out at night. It might get cold or wet or be hurt in a road accident.

Playing

Cats and kittens love to play and explore.

They will play with you …

Be careful if the cat sees your fingers moving. It might go for them instead of the toy.

…or by themselves.

Don't let your cat play with small things like marbles, which it could swallow, or sharp things, like scissors or needles.

Kittens learn to hunt when they play. They learn to hide in wait, listen for their prey and then track it down. They practise killing animals by jumping on toys.

1. First they watch the prey. They will sometimes do this for a long time.

2. Then they slowly stalk the prey. They move without making a sound.

3. Suddenly they pounce on the prey and bite it to kill it. Often they play with the prey afterwards.

Playing with your cat

Cats like toys that make a noise, such as crumpled up newspaper. Don't frighten the cat with a loud or sudden noise.

Don't leave wool or string lying around. Your cat may swallow some or get its claws caught.

If you leave an empty box or a paper bag on the floor, your cat may like to dive inside it to explore. Don't let the cat play with plastic bags. It could suffocate.

Cats love climbing. They have a good sense of balance. Their tail helps them to balance.

Strong claws to grip branch.

Let the cat catch the toy from time to time otherwise it will get bored.

Training

Cats will do what they like. They cannot be trained like dogs. But there are some things that they can learn, such as using a litter tray or a cat flap or coming when you call their name.

Kittens are trained by their mother to use a litter tray.

Show your kitten where its new tray is. Put it in the tray after meals and in the morning and at night.

Cats are very clean animals. When they go to the lavatory, they use a hole that they have dug. Then they cover it up. Clean out the litter tray every week and change the litter every day. Then wash your hands. If you want to train your cat to use a garden, move the litter tray gradually nearer the door. After a few days, put the tray outside the door.

Cat flap fixed in a door.

When your kitten is about 4 months old, train it to use a cat flap. Put the kitten just outside before it has its meal. Let it see its food through the open flap. When it comes through the flap, give it the food. Do this before each meal until it learns to use the flap.

It is easier to stop your cat from learning bad habits than it is to teach it new ones. If you find the cat doing something you don't want it to do, say "no" firmly and move the cat away.
Never hit your cat.

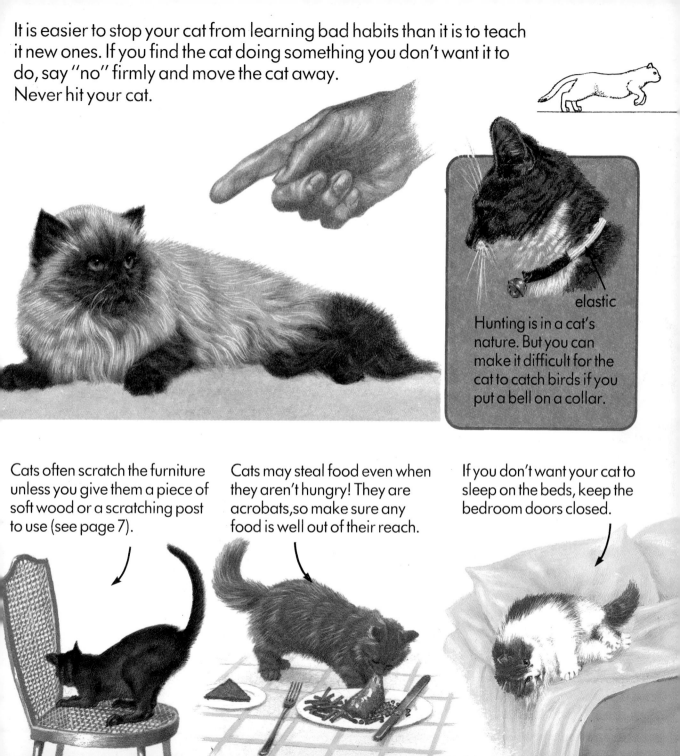

elastic

Hunting is in a cat's nature. But you can make it difficult for the cat to catch birds if you put a bell on a collar.

Cats often scratch the furniture unless you give them a piece of soft wood or a scratching post to use (see page 7).

Cats may steal food even when they aren't hungry! They are acrobats, so make sure any food is well out of their reach.

If you don't want your cat to sleep on the beds, keep the bedroom doors closed.

Handling your cat

Your kitten may miss its mother at first. It will enjoy the comfort of being held and stroked. Always handle a cat or kitten gently.

Use both your hands to hold your cat or kitten. Put one hand under the front paws and use the other hand to support the cat's bottom.

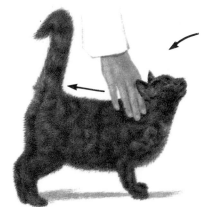

Talk to your kitten and use its name. Stroke it gently in the same direction that the fur grows.

Your kitten may let you know when it wants to be stroked, to play or to sleep. Don't bother it too much or it will get overtired and angry.

Your cat will come to you when it wants your company. When it rubs against your legs like this, it is saying "I feel friendly"

When you play with your kitten, don't leave it in a high place. It may hurt itself when it tries to get down. Never drop it from a height either.

16

Grooming

Cats need grooming. Brush your kitten for short periods each day so that it gets used to being groomed.

If you have a long-haired cat, brush and comb it every day. Remove things caught in the fur before they make a tangle. Don't pull knots – be patient and tease them out slowly. Short-haired cats need brushing when they are moulting.

Brush the cat all over in the direction that the fur grows.

Washing

Cats spend a lot of time cleaning themselves. They don't need baths and hate water. Their rough tongue acts like a comb. They use their front paw like a sponge to wash their face.

Cats can reach almost any part of their body, because they are so flexible.

Kittens soon start to wash themselves like their mother.

17

Leaving home

Travelling

Most cats hate travelling and will try to escape. It is a good idea to get a cat used to travelling while it is still a kitten. You will need a strong box or basket to carry your cat in.

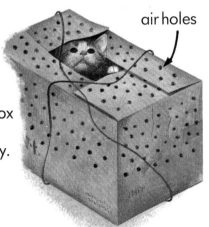

air holes

A cat can struggle out of a cardboard box if the box isn't tied up properly. The box may also fall apart if it rains.

The collar must have some elastic so the cat has a chance to wriggle free if the collar gets caught.

Disc or tube for your name and address.

A collar like this will help to stop the cat getting lost. Get the cat used to the collar before you go on a journey.

Cats are sometimes less frightened in wire baskets because they can see what is going on. They get plenty of air too.

Inside the basket

newspaper

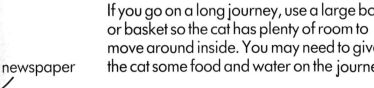

newspaper

If you go on a long journey, use a large box or basket so the cat has plenty of room to move around inside. You may need to give the cat some food and water on the journey.

Holidays

When you go on holiday, your cat will want to stay at home.

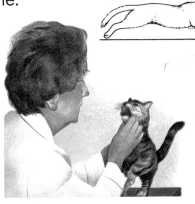

Some catteries put several cats together. Some give your cat its own area.

You may be able to get a neighbour or friend to come in every day to feed your cat and check that it is safe and well. If you can't do this, or if you are going away for more than a week or so, take your cat to a cattery. Choose one well before you go away as the good ones are usually very busy at holiday time.

The people at the cattery will check that your cat is healthy before they let it stay. They may ask for vaccination certificates (see page 21).

Moving house

If you move to a new home, make a fuss of your cat. Make sure its own toys and bowls are easy for it to find. As your cat gets older, it will be more upset by moving and take longer to settle in.

Keep your cat indoors for a few days until it gets to know the new home. Then let it out to explore just before mealtimes. It will soon come back to eat rather than going too far away and getting lost.

19

Your cat's health

A healthy cat looks alert, with bright eyes and a clean, glossy coat. It eats well and spends a lot of time washing and grooming. If you see a change in the way your cat looks, eats, drinks or sleeps this could mean it isn't feeling well. Sickness, diarrhoea, coughing and sneezing can be signs of illness.

Chewing grass

Cats will eat grass sometimes. This can make them vomit and helps them to get rid of balls of fur in their stomach. Town cats that don't have a garden or yard should have their own patch of grass in a window box or flower pot.

Small animals, such as fleas, mites or worms may live on your cat's skin or inside its body. They may make the cat feel ill.

Fleas

Fleas can live on a cat's skin. If your cat has fleas, it will scratch its body a lot. Brush the cat over a pale surface. Then take the cat away and sprinkle water on the surface. If red specks appear, your cat has fleas. Buy some flea powder and follow the instructions. Clean the cat's bed and the carpets thoroughly.

Ear Mites

Mites can live in the wax inside a cat's ear. The cat will scratch its ears and shake its head. Don't touch the ears as they are very delicate. Take the cat to a vet.

Worms

All kittens should be given a medicine for roundworms. Adult cats may get tapeworms. Go to your vet for medicines.

20

Going to the vet

The vet can give your cat injections that will help to stop it getting some serious illnesses. This is called "vaccination". Ask your vet about vaccinations while your cat is still a kitten. If you think your cat is ill or has been injured, ask an adult to help you take it to the vet. Some diseases can kill a cat in just a few days.

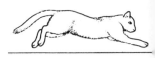

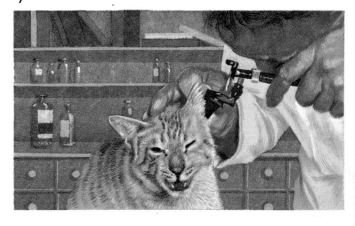

When your cat is ill, put it gently in its travelling box and take it to the vet. If the cat tries to scratch or bite you, ask an adult to help you wrap it in a blanket or towel.

The vet will examine your cat and tell you what is wrong. This cat has something in its ears. Ask the vet how to look after your cat at home when it is ill. Let the cat rest quietly.

Giving pills or medicine

Often the vet will give you pills or medicine to give your cat at home.

It isn't easy to give pills or medicine to cats. You can try mixing a crushed pill or some medicine with the cats' food but they often won't eat it.

Ask your vet how to give pills to a cat. Don't do this by yourself. An adult must help you otherwise you may get bitten.

21

Cats and kittens

A female cat can start having kittens when she is about six months old. She could have three litters every year with up to six kittens in each litter.

It is very difficult to find good homes for so many kittens. It is best to take your cat to the vet when she is about six months old to have an operation called spaying. This will stop her having kittens.

A male cat should have an operation called neutering when he is about six months old. This will stop him being the father of any kittens. A neutered cat is usually quieter and more home-loving.

Vets will shave the area where they operate.

Some male cats get fatter after they are neutered.

If a female cat is **not** spayed, she will behave strangely from time to time. She will call for a male in a loud, wailing voice. She will also rub against things to leave her scent for a male cat.

If a male cat is **not** neutered, he often spends a lot of time out of doors. He may fight other male cats and come home dirty and perhaps wounded. He will leave a strong scent in the house.

A female cat may roll on the ground to attract a male cat.

The male cat that wins the fight may mate with the female.

22

When your cat has kittens

After a female cat has mated, baby kittens may start to form inside her. This is called being pregnant. Don't pick her up unless you have to and handle her very gently.

If your cat is pregnant, her nipples will be swollen and pinker than usual.

Her tummy will get larger as the kittens grow inside her.

A pregnant cat will become very hungry and needs much more food. She may also need cod-liver oil and extra vitamins.

Your cat will be ready to give birth about nine weeks after mating. She will look for a warm, safe place to make a nest.

Cats are good mothers and do not usually need help when they give birth. It is best to watch from nearby so you can call the vet if there any problems. As soon as they are born, the kittens crawl to their mother's nipples to suck milk. Don't handle the kittens until their eyes are open.

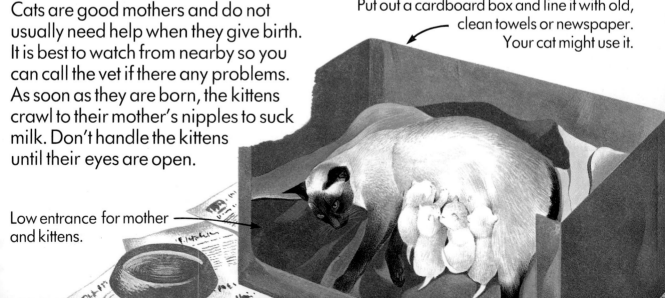

Put out a cardboard box and line it with old, clean towels or newspaper. Your cat might use it.

Low entrance for mother and kittens.

Picture puzzle

There are 13 cats hidden in this picture.
Can you find them all?